Michelangela and Debuts

Discovering the Self

Joan Thomson Kretschmer

• Chicago •

Michelangela and Debuts
Discovering the Self
Joan Thomson Kretschmer

Published by
Joshua Tree Publishing
• Chicago •
JoshuaTreePublishing.com

13-Digit ISBN: 978-1-941049-76-1

Cover Image Credit: © poriaco

Disclaimer:
This is a work of fiction. Names, characters, places, and incidents are the product of the author's imagination or have been used fictitiously. Any resemblance to actual persons, living or dead, events, locales or organizations is entirely coincidental.

Printed in the United States of America

Dedication

*This book is dedicated to my sons,
Keith Joel Thomson and Elliot Robert Thomson.*

Michelangela

Long ago, a tiny spider, Michelangela, was born in a dark, cavernous mansion.

A solitary old man rattled through its half-empty rooms, cane tap-tapping, sparking swirls of dust. His days melted away in napping, shuffling up and down the long, winding staircases, and nibbling meager meals in the paint-peeled kitchen. To his poor, tired feet, short distances were marathons, and hazy cataracts dimmed his gray eyes.

As years vanished, he showed *absolutely no interest* in housekeeping and shunned all visitors, except his only daughter, who came every Sunday with fresh food and clean clothing.

"What can I do for you, Dad?" she asked in a lilting, smiling voice.

"Nothing, thanks! I'm quite content," was his usual response. If she opened the creaky broom closet and reached for the rusty handle of the ancient feather duster, he would stop her abruptly.

"You're not a scullery maid!" he snapped, in a whispering trace of his once strong and commanding tone. "Everything is just fine the way it is. Go along and have fun; don't worry about me."

Because of the old man's lifestyle, every spider in town was attracted to his home. The large, spacious rooms and dark hallways were havens from icy cold winters, drenching spring rains, blistering hot summers, and the constant nuisance of falling autumn leaves.

It is no surprise, therefore, that Michelangela's life was the happiest a little spider could dream of—or imagine. From the moment she opened her tiny eyes, she discovered a kind of Spider Heaven: a world of enormous, elaborate webs and sympathetic, kindred spirits.

Her earliest memory was her cradle: a supportive network of suspended strong threads prepared by her mother for her brand-new little body. Michelangela's first tenuous steps were on hairsbreadth, curving pathways; and as soon as her footing was secure, she scurried down fine-spun highways and filamentary byways. Little by little, she became daring and left nearby familiar perches for far-flung webs.

Many wonderful hours and days were spent swinging, gyrating and dancing in a series of miniature tightrope acts. Anyone would have admired her agility, as she maneuvered like a lithe, young monkey, flying through the air, swooping from one flossy thread to the next. Skittering along, like the sailors of old, charging up a vast network of interlocking ropes, she hurried to the very top and back down again—eventually landing upright on at least several of her many feet.

Michelangela believed that her mother must be the most amazing creature on earth. Who else could embroider such luxuriant, complicated webs and round them out with nooks for climbing and sliding? And in such profusion!

Her mother's web-work was everywhere: decorating windowpanes, floating from antique lamps, outlining the big old arms of dining room chairs, drifting gracefully down from doorways. Her original, dazzling patterns ornamented the crystal chandeliers, and her feathery filigree draped elegantly across floor-to-ceiling bookcases.

Why her mother even knew ways to create dark, inaccessible corners so that you could play hide-and seek all day long—and never be found!

Michelangela watched her mother spinning for hours, sometimes for entire days. If only she could make webs like those! Try as she might, little Michelangela was simply all feet, at first. No sooner did she create a thread, then she was all caught up in it, her own prisoner. In an instant, with infinite patience and kindness, her mother stopped whatever she was doing to rescue and disentangle her well-intentioned offspring.

Michelangela studied her mother's every movement, knowing that she was in the presence of a master. Then she huffed and puffed, until at last she was able to put two threads together, three, and then four. "Like this," her mother would show her, handing down her craft to the next generation.

The baby spider practiced with a passion; dedication and zeal made her a model apprentice, as she developed technique, expertise, special tricks, and eventually her art. Michelangela's life was engrossing: she thrived on the consuming challenge of web-manufacture and the busy, merry little world of the spider-filled household.

There were so many friends and so much to do. Time was always too short, and days flew by all too quickly, but very happily. What else could a little spider want?

One New Year's Day, everything changed abruptly, and her peaceful, productive, rich life was altered catastrophically. The old man went up for a nap and simply did not shuffle down again.

His daughter arrived that very day. By the end of the week, she had supervised the removal of his furniture and belongings and brought a cleaning crew to dust and vacuum. Each morning, she opened the heavy wooden doors for another group of men, who spent hours washing the hundreds of windows. Buckets and brushes came in the hands of a flock of painters, who moved in to spend a month sloshing paint in every direction, along every wall, into every crevice.

Webs vanished and the spider community hid from the many feet of assorted real estate agents, who were destroying the accustomed serenity.

By spring, the house was sold to a new family with screaming, fighting, kicking and yelping children. Horror of horrors, the lady of the house could not stand spiders!

"Kill that thing!" she bellowed the day the moving trucks arrived, lifting her mammoth foot to squash Michelangela's mother, who luckily escaped.

"Get that one," she snarled, the next morning, during the unpacking. A few minutes later, she was back again, attacking Michelangela with a long wooden broom.

Fortunately, our heroine was unharmed, but she suffered many more incidents of harassment. Every few moments, there was another hysterical family member shrieking and chasing yet another innocent spider.

When one of Michelangela's little legs was badly bruised by the new owner's sharp heel, and emotional life was reaching a feverish pitch of high anxiety, the spiders convened to make a plan to deal with the new reality. There was no question, everyone agreed: time had come to move. As soon as possible. Immediately.

That very night, at dark, they fled: a little troop trailing off down the muddy road, in a terrifying storm. Occasional bursts of lightning provided the only illumination; and the sheets of hard, cold, rain created serious flooding conditions for each and every one of them, no matter how old or experienced.

Hail thundered down, bouncing in every direction, threatening life and limb. The wind howled, shook trees, hurled branches to the ground, and dropped unexpected, mountainous obstacles everywhere.

Michelangela crept along, trying to avoid flying debris. What if she were to drown in roadside seas? She could see nothing in the pitch-blackness, although she heard voices receding in the distance. Suddenly, the others were gone, and she was all alone. When the sky blazed for an instant, she noticed a group of boulders and ran for cover, slipping and sliding into a warm, dry niche.

As she huddled in a corner, shaking with fear, a tiny, steamy spider-tear wet her cheek and fell silently to the ground. "What is happening to me? What should I do? What *can* I do?" she cried, but when she called for help, only her voice echoed, bouncing off the boulders. Going out was far too dangerous. Could anyone else hear her or help her? Where was her mother?

The storm raged and tore at the sky, and she stayed hidden, drying off little by little, getting very hungry. As her tired body grew heavy, she snuggled up against a soft mound of moss and fell into a deep sleep.

The sun was shining brightly, when she woke up. Timidly, she crawled out and looked around, but had absolutely no idea where she was. There was a very small white wooden house in the distance, so she started toward it.

Standing at the edge of the road, she looked up the long slate flagstone path to the front steps. Slowly, she edged past the flowers lining either side. Black and yellow butterflies flitted across blue-purple pansies, lavender tulips, golden daffodils, and orange primrose. The sweet, heady perfume of white hyacinths was in the air. It was a cheerful, welcoming place.

Coming close to the small gray wooden door, our tiny adventurer noticed a wreath of herbs laced with ivy and dotted with miniature, dried pomegranates. She stopped to admire the red clay pots brimming with pink geraniums on the little porch. The two windows, on each side of the doorway, were teeming with velvety, crimson gloxinia, waxy, Persian red begonias, and a tiny jungle of shiny green plants. Michelangela had never seen such an abundance of growing things. When a small boy opened the door, she darted in and was almost killed, as the screen slammed behind him. She raced up the leg of a nearby table and hid quietly, beneath the top.

Now what?

She listened, waited and watched. During the next few hours, she thought about the changes in her life. The truth was sinking in: her mother was gone, she was alone, and she had lost everyone she had known and loved.

In a state of shock, fighting disbelief, Michelangela was impaled with fear. Her thoughts turned back to her happy home. After all, her mother had prepared her for a spider's life. So, she began to do what she had learned: spin and weave—hoping her work would attract attention and make new friends.

She selected the best place for her debut, the kitchen doorway, a spot no one could miss; and she spent the night preparing a web that anyone and everyone could adore. Then she waited for the members of the household to wake up—with positive reviews.

Before the family sat down to breakfast, there was another broom, sweeping away her work and bearing down on her. Michelangela slipped out the open window, running as fast as her little legs would carry her, and fled.

Over and over, the story was repeated. An exhausting day or sleepless night of traveling was followed by taking shelter in someone's home. Within hours of making her first web, she was discovered and pursued relentlessly.

Poor soul. Small brooms, big sticks, large dusters, rolled newspapers, rusty hangers, giant feet, all were her persecutors.

One day she almost suffocated, when a little boy trapped her in a cup. Fortunately, he lost interest in his prisoner, who crept away weakened, crawled under a bed of blood-red impatiens, and fainted.

"Why me? What did I do to deserve this? Where is my darling, extraordinary mother? Where are my friends? Why was I ejected from my warm, safe, protected home into such a cold, unfeeling, miserable world?" she sobbed, lost in self-pity.

"What am I supposed to be doing with my life?" she wondered, reviewing the dreadful, life endangering, shocking series of events. "What is this world all about?" she asked herself over and over. "Where can I find peace?"

But she had no clear answers, no friendly advice, only constant turmoil and more perplexing questions. She was forced to keep going, to press on, to search for as yet unknown, unrevealed, uncertain solutions.

Traveling across the countryside, Michelangela made a joyous discovery: spending time outdoors was a source of great pleasure for her. Her spirits were refreshed by kaleidoscopic vistas in an ever-changing landscape. Her soul was invigorated by the apparently endless variety of colored flowers, by the thick pungent pine groves, and by the ruddy Japanese maples, grand old oak trees, and fleecy weeping willows. How beautiful were the graceful dogwoods bulging with sensuous pink and white blossoms!

Warm sunshine soothed her tired back, and an infinite, expansive blue sky inspired her. Often, when she rested, she followed the movements of the puffy white clouds strung above her eyes. What wonderful shapes they formed! How they fired her imagination, as stories of wispy animals, stealthy monsters, and monumental palaces tumbled about in her mind. Each new day, the splendors of nature were soothing antidotes to her pain, suffering, and longing.

How free she felt, when she could see to the end of the horizon, unhampered by constricting walls and ceilings. "Wheee!" she sang gleefully, as she stretched her little legs as far as they could go and scooted along happily.

After living indoors, staying outside was new and a bit frightening. Especially since her mother had always emphasized the security and comfort of the old mansion, protected from the elements and from stress.

But now that life was a series of mad-dashes-for-safety, Michelangela had to consider every possible alternative. Expansive fields and large gardens had rocks and bushes with safe hiding places, where she could protect herself. The serene countryside had neither brooms nor the myriad of other assorted weapons with which she had become all too familiar.

She began to dream of spinning to her heart's content where no one would bother her. Gradually, she calmed down, reassured her beating heart, and started to search for an appropriate location. The more she understood her needs, the more she wished for a beautiful garden, since she had grown to love flowers so very much.

One warm May day, as she ambled down the road, she spotted the gray stone turrets of a large castle towering on a majestic mountainside. Acres of lush, formal gardens rose from the road, up the incline, to the top. A sinuous drive was edged with hundreds of stately, arching elms. To the left, the hillside was blanketed with red, white, and pink azaleas, as far as the eye could see. To the right, topiary animals lumbered along in silent spaces, and a trellis-covered walkway curved in geometric patterns around perennial gardens.

Could this be the place? It seemed to have everything: natural splendor to soothe her harried soul and charming, covered nooks to protect her worn-out body. But recent experiences had made her wary and cautious . . .

Michelangela trudged up the slope, stopping under a large rectangle of trimmed bushes. What a peaceful spot: red and white-water lilies drifted quietly on the pale blue surface of a small pond. Black-orange goldfish gleamed as they darted around a small island, where a bronze boy bathed in a misty waterfall. Along the path, white benches invited the visitor to sit and look—or think. In the farthest corner, a velvety gray cat pounced onto an antique swing, snuggled in the slice of sun cutting through a latticed roof, and covered his eyes dreamily with his right paw.

Through the bushes, Michelangela saw a sturdy stone shed surrounded by large planters. She crept to the doorway and peeked inside, where wooden toolboxes, bicycles, a croquet set, and assorted games were stored. A new home—out of harm's way.

She had found what she needed: cover from storms, yards of green leafy backdrop for elegant webs, and long borders chock full of spectacular flowers. As she entered the shed, she was greeted by the delicious odor of the lily-of-the-valley encircling the entire foundation.

In a warm, dry spot on the highest shelf, near the ceiling, Michelangela went to sleep, safe for the first time in months—or had it been years?

At the crack of dawn, she raced out to see the sunrise and to explore her new surroundings. The melodious chatter of hundreds of birds caressed her ears, sweet breezes blew, and the animal world buzzed with activity. The view down the hillside and across the valley would have been breathtaking to any spectator.

Jumping onto a large bush, she began to spin one of her favorite patterns. The sun climbed higher and higher into the sky, and the leaves reflected snatches of its fire. Michelangela evaluated her work, touching up here and there. Once again, after seemingly endless agony, she was appreciative of the gift of life.

That morning, animals of all sizes and kinds came to greet her. The Prince would be coming soon, they said, with anticipation. He arrived every day at 10 to sit by the pool and draw. She was in *his garden*, they explained and described a unique, remarkable, esteemed man who revered living creatures and nature's marvels.

Minutes later, leaves rustled, and goldfish splashed in the pool, as a handsome young man, in his mid-20s, appeared with a sketchpad under his arm. He sat down near the water's edge, and Michelangela watched his face and his movements. He appeared to be the gentle, kind, sensitive soul the animals had prepared her for. She relaxed and was not afraid.

For several hours, he drew, calmly and quietly. As he was leaving, he noticed her web. "Why I've never seen anything like that," he muttered to himself, looking at it from this angle and that. He sat down again, on the closest bench, opened the sketchpad, and tried to copy what she had created. "What a beautiful form," he mumbled, as he tried to imitate the intricate structure. When he was finished, he smiled and walked away, looking very satisfied.

Michelangela couldn't believe her eyes or her glowing heart! Someone actually appreciated what she did. SHE FELT WONDERFUL!

The next morning, she was up before dawn. She would outdo yesterday's efforts. He hadn't seen anything yet!

The Prince came early, while the dew was still fresh, glistening in little globules on the day-old web. Michelangela had just completed a new one inches below. Small beads of water rested gently on her gossamer framework. As the Prince looked closely, each drop seemed to contain a diminutive rainbow. He stood in quiet awe.

Once again, he opened the sketchpad to capture what he saw. "Nothing can reproduce this," he blurted, with frustration, after trying every color combination in his box. He left abruptly and returned a few minutes later, with members of his family trailing behind.

"Look at the delicacy, the elaborate design, the astonishing ornamentation," he began, with breathless excitement. His hands flew, tracing circles within circles, etching spiraling ovals in the air, pointing to the subtle details of the ethereal maze. Everyone agreed it was "perfection."

The Prince was inspiring Michelangela. Each day she spun with greater and greater abandon, highlighting the greenery with new shapes and wondrous arches. And each day, he came to study, savor and preserve her forms in his notebook.

She grew happier and happier, as she became the talk of the local animal kingdom and of the castle's inhabitants. The Prince filled sketchbook after sketchbook with the products of her imagination.

It was a Mutual Inspiration Society, as they stimulated and enriched each other's creativity. In a unique way, they were communicating with one another, and a curious affection grew between them. She looked forward to his visits; he couldn't wait to get up in the morning to see what she was doing.

If only she could speak to him, she thought, but she did not know how. She addressed him with her art; he responded with his. He was often moved to tears by the outpourings of her heart; she soared to new heights because of his observations.

Unspoken utterances were met with mirrors of her soul. Inarticulate delivery was matched by paper discourses. Silently, she gave expression to her deepest emotions; dutifully, he noted them, preserving their transmutations long after the original threads had vanished.

Mutual inspiration grew to mutual adoration. Thus they lived in parallel . . .

One day, he broke the silence and spoke.

"How you have changed my life and my way of seeing. I can't believe that a single living creature could have such a dramatic impact on me. You touch the deepest part of my being, and I don't know how to thank you—or to tell you. Even if you could understand what I say, there are no words to describe my feelings. You magical, minuscule little organism, you have drawn me into your intricate, imaginative world of beauty, and I am your captive."

She listened with rapt attention and her heart prodded her:

"I wish I could make you hear me. I am so happy when you are happy. If only I could let you know what you mean to me. It is so wonderful that we are friends, but we are so many worlds apart. How can I reach you?"

"Try," he answered gently.

She was astounded. Her heard her voice *and understood her.* That was not possible!

She climbed up near her most recent web and let him see her. He reached out gently and guided her carefully onto his hand.

"Such a tiny dot performing such sorcery! Such a charming enchantress."

(See Endings 1,2,3, and 4.)

Ending #1

The first words she uttered were, "Thank you, my lord."

They spoke for a few moments, the first of many conversations.

Each day he came to sit beside her, and for many years now they have talked and worked in the peace and quiet of that lovely setting.

He has become world famous for his drawings, which are sought after by private collectors and exhibited in important museums throughout the world. Docents lecture about them, and art historians rave about their web-like patterns. Critics fill reams of paper and columns of magazines with talk of the fine geometry and delicate pen strokes. But they cannot really understand the Prince's art, although they make great pretense.

"The painterly chiaroscuro is enhanced by the quintessentially baroque perspective, but one is reminded of the Renaissance Dureresque style in black-and-white contrasting flow of line," wrote the eminent Mr. Moe Vision recently in the prestigious periodical, *Art Gibberish.*

Everyone in the Prince's castle and gardens laughed.

Only those living there know the truth.

If you were to visit the castle today, at the right hour, you might see Michelangela spinning happily near the Prince's new sign: Artist at Work.

Or you might be lucky enough to see some of her little apprentices studying. You see, she has children and grandchildren now. Like her mother, she has handed her love of beauty down to the next, *and the next* generation. Every day, they demonstrate their inherited talents and family heritage. Like all artists, they simply have to work; the necessity comes from deep inside. And nothing stops them.

Ending #2

Suddenly in her place stood a beautiful woman, with long flowing black hair and *very long legs*. Michelangela, the spider, was gone.

"Fate brought you to this spot," he said, gently. "You were imprisoned by a wicked witch, who was jealous of your mother's beauty and talent. To punish her, the witch cursed you both to lead the life of bugs, chased from place to place, given no rest."

"You could only be released after a complex series of trials. First, you were forced to use your talents to survive. Second, you had to be appreciated by a man living in a remote corner of the earth—someone exceedingly difficult, almost impossible for you to find. Last but not least, you had to trust that man, show him your soul, put yourself in his hands, and have no fear of him."

"Obviously, the possibility of your release was exceedingly remote. Even I didn't understand it, until the moment I held you on my palm. Then I remembered a story I was told as a child."

"Touch my soul and see how it feels, "Michelangela said, startling him. "Put your hand deep inside its hollows and curve your fingers into its velvety folds. Curl yourself into its black, deep vast arches. You are welcome there, my love."

He watched her as she moved close to him and touched his cheeks with her fingertips. "I dare you to take me into your gifted hands, my darling," she continued. "Knead my soul; smooth out the pain that was embedded in your place. Stretch the folds, remove the scars of the years without you. Obliterate the old wounds with your love."

As he gathered her into his arms, he answered quietly, his lips close to her ear: "My soul has spent many weary hours waiting for you, many unhappy moments wondering if you would ever come. Now it can rest."

Michelangela and the Prince lived happily together, finding loving refuge from the world: she enhanced the lives of those around them, and he loved everything she said and did!

He became world famous for his drawings, which are sought after by private collectors and exhibited in important museums throughout the world. Docents lecture about them, and art historians rave about their web-like patterns. Critics fill reams of paper and columns of magazines with talk of the fine geometry and delicate pen strokes. But they cannot really understand the Prince's art, although they make great pretense.

"The painterly chiaroscuro is enhanced by the quintessentially baroque perspective, but one is reminded of the Renaissance Dureresque style in the black-and white contrasting flow of line," wrote the eminent Mr. Moe Vision in the prestigious periodical, *Art Gibberish.*

Everyone in the Prince's castle and gardens laughed. Only those living there knew the truth:

Michelangela was "the woman behind the man."

Ending #3

Suddenly, in his place, there was a handsome spider, with very long legs. The Prince, the person, was gone.

"Fate brought me to this spot," Michelangela said, softly. "When you held me, everything became clear. A wicked witch cursed you to live as a human being. I was selected to release you. But your freedom was inextricably linked with mine. Both of us had to pass through a series of difficult, perhaps impossible tests, and each of us had to enhance the world around us."

He listened attentively, moving closer to her, stretching and testing his many new legs.

"First, you had to create a place of extraordinary beauty, an environment of peace and tranquility, where nature's creatures could live in harmony. A spot where the air is clean, the water unpolluted, and flowers grow in profusion. That was very unlikely in a world where human beings spend every working hour destroying the visual purity of this planet—in the names of progress, modern life, and necessity."

"Second, you had to welcome any creature who wanted to live there, without conditions, regardless of the opinion of others. Third, you had to open your mind to the miraculous activity of the various inhabitants and communicate your sense of wonder to others. If you could see in a new way and help ordinary mortals to appreciate what you were seeing, then you could be saved."

He moved closer, until their legs were intertwined, and their bodies touched.

"While you were enduring your trials, I was chased from place to place, given no rest, forced to use my every wit to survive. You were in some distant corner of the earth, and I had to reach you. I was driven to earn your appreciation, and I had to learn to trust you, show you my soul, and put myself in your hands without fear."

"It is a miracle that we are together at last," she concluded joyously, "but I'm exhausted by the long, lonely journey."

They spoke for a few moments, intimately and lovingly, the first of many conversations.

"At last we have found comfort," he said, reassuringly, gathering her close to him, protectively.

For the rest of their days, they lived and worked happily in the splendor and quiet of that lovely setting, as companions, friends, and lovers.

Ending #4

Michelangela is invited to join the Female Spider Support Group, where she discusses standing on her own many feet.

March 9, 1991.

Debuts

One day, the stork brought an unusual infant to the tiny town of Somewhere.

Amore was the first baby girl in the community in a decade, interrupting a string of little boys. Local folk had almost forgotten about little girls. The General Store on Main Street had sold its last pink layette and closed its Little Women's Shoppe long ago. The children's department was brimming with baseball caps, football shirts, fly-front pants, miniature cars, trucks and other accoutrements designed to develop a young mind for the onerous burdens of adult masculinity.

Gossips agreed that Amore was exceptionally beautiful, and many pairs of attentive eyes peered into her carriage to study the shock of brown curls framing her porcelain white skin, ruby-red lips, and hazel eyes.

Professor Blythe, the neighborhood art critic, compared her to the cherubic angels floating on cotton-white clouds in the paintings of the Old Masters. Friends seemed to be helplessly addicted to pinching her miniature rosy cheeks and to watching her chubby little arms and legs bob up and down.

Her parents, Mr. and Mrs. Adore, invited everyone to a celebratory welcoming party on the Village Green, where the High School Band marched, threading its way through the entire population of 613 residents. Sitting in the freshly painted white gazebo, tapping his foot and strumming his guitar, was Methuselah, the well-known old-timer. He was joined by the Only Quartet which played requests for old favorites.

Gifts were piled on top of each other to form a pink pyramid, with delicate bows wafting in the gentle May breezes. Many had been imported from miles away, because it was quite a feat to find soft, feminine presents close to home. Guests had traveled great distances to shop in far-off towns, where little girls were more plentiful.

Crib and carriage were inundated with coverlets in pinks and reds of every shade and hue. Sheets were splashed with salmon-pink elephants, crimson giraffes, and scarlet bears. Amore's food dribbled onto milk-white organdy bibs decorated with cherry chipmunks, coral-colored whales, and vermilion dogs.

And her mother stored her fleecy sweaters, little red velvet dresses, carnation pink hair bows, and white lace socks—for use at future, special occasions.

Never did a girl receive so many dolls: bride dolls, collector dolls, big dolls, little dolls. Dolls to dress, to feed, to bathe. Dolls who cried, sang, recited poetry—and even an adolescent one which talked back.

How many children in human history have received so much attention?

Mrs. Adore beamed, declaring herself to be "the happiest woman on earth" and hovered over the most minute details of her baby's new precious life, watching Amore's every move, introducing her to the joys of bathing in her little tub. At the slightest cry, she would scoop her infant up in her arms, soothe her tiny body, and shower her with love.

Like every good, conscientious mother, she made an appointment for Amore's first checkup. Dr. Dedicated, the pediatrician, did all the routine things—weight, temperature, and shots—but suddenly, his face clouded. As he listened to the new little heart, his nose wrinkled, and a troubled look contorted his face. Again and again, he put his stethoscope against the little chest, listening, listening.

"Something is very odd," he began, after several hour-long-moments. "There is a faint murmur," he added gravely, "I've never heard anything like this, and I don't have the slightest idea what it is."

Amore's mother froze in her seat. Her body stiffened involuntarily, and her stomach churned. Her mind began to race ahead of his words, imagining the worst, conjuring up the most horrifying scenarios.

"Give me a little time to investigate," he said, in a soothing, calming tone, trying not to alarm the new mother. "I'd like to do some reading and consult my colleagues. Meanwhile, Amore seems to be in perfect health. Don't worry; it won't help, you know. I'll call you as soon as I have some information."

The light was on in his study the entire night, as he leafed through his medical books and journals. Sadly, he found no answers. His recommendation: "Take the baby to The Greatest Medical Center in the country to be examined by the most eminent, illustrious, and experienced physicians."

So off went Amore, bundled up in her new pink wardrobe, nestled in her parents' arms. The Greatest's wise men were waiting in an impressive, memorable row to study the diminutive patient.

Dr. Grand, the first and tallest, bent himself pretzel-like to place his large ear against her petite chest. "The sound seems so far away, I can scarcely hear it."

"It's beyond me," chimed in the small, wee voice of Dr. Little, the second and the shortest, who was world-famous for his specialization in midgets, the microscopic, and the minuscule.

"This is certainly a meaty, tough, weighty problem," ruminated Dr. Chub, who weighed at least 300 pounds and appeared to have three chins hanging on his turkey-neck. "Maybe not a full-blown, monumental heart murmur, but a case of hefty proportions, if you'll pardon the colossal pun."

Dr. Slight, the thinnest, struggled to find the appropriate terms to immortalize himself in the

Leading Learned Medical Journal: "The sound is meagre but not trivial."

"Why I never!" droned Dr. Venerable, the oldest and most conservative. "I thought I'd seen and heard *everything* in my life!" he mumbled, scratching his long white beard.

"Like a drum played in a tank full of water," thundered Dr. Bee-Bop, the percussionist of the Physicians' Orchestra.

"This is priceless," leered Dr. Greed, rubbing his hands. "You should have the help, ideas, and recommendations of the world's medical community at no cost, free of charge. Amore's may be a historic case," he added with excitement, preparing his bill.

Amazingly, the Greatest's best minds had no clarifying thoughts. There were the experts, standing for hours, stethoscopes dangling from their necks; but no one had ever described such a problem before, and none of them could explain it now.

"We are stumped! It is a sonic novelty," they concluded, in a chorus of perplexed voices. "Take Amore abroad, to The Annual World Conference of Vacationing Physicians which is meeting at this very moment," they advised.

So Amore's father gathered up the pink bundle and headed off, with his wife and Dr. Dedicated hurrying along beside him.

At the Conference, she became a major attraction. More probing, pondering and pontificating, but no answers.

Despite her travels and the many hands, ears, and instruments pressing against her Lilliputian heart, Amore thrived. She was eating heartily, growing rapidly, smiling from ear to ear, and babbling baby talk.

"There doesn't seem to be any negative effect on the baby," bellowed Dr. Pretense, the renowned know-it-all and politically astute President of the Annual World Conference.

"People have lived with heart murmurs," he roared to the thousands of doctors lolling under striped umbrellas on a vast sandy beach.

"Perhaps nothing will develop. We can only wait and see . . .

Meanwhile, she should lead a normal life. Dr. Dedicated will supervise the case, record her progress, and keep us informed."

The Adore parents were somewhat relieved, although they had hoped for an explanation. Their state of shock was subsiding to an ever-present, undercurrent of worry, but they were adjusting to a perplexing, frustrating situation . . .

Back home, people had been talking of almost nothing else. Amore's condition was whispered about on porch stoops, in the Greasy Spoon, and at the dentist's office. Speculation ebbed and flowed: Was it a heart murmur? A rare communicable disease? An incurable weakness? Daily, a line of nosey residents waited at the one-room Post Office to read medical analyses the moment they arrived in the mail.

"Everything is under control," the medical-conference-hopping-parents summarized to a waiting, expectant crowd.

"Whew," was the general sigh of relief uttered with such unanimity that it shook the branches and blew the leaves of nearby trees like a great gust of wind. Life returned to normal.

Nothing seemed out of the ordinary during the next few years. Amore cooed, gooed, chattered, and explored the world around her; she seemed to be a healthy child. To her parents' great pleasure, she tumbled, fumbled, bumbled and rumbled through toddlerhood—without exceptional problems. Their fears were fading . . .

Life was a constant delight for Amore. Everything fascinated her: she studied faces, imitated new words, plucked flowers, chased animals, and splashed in puddles. Pots and pans were her rhythm section and drawers her treasure chests. Nothing missed her scrutiny: she examined every item in the medicine cabinet, danced to the swishing of the washer, hummed along with the vibrating dryer, and immersed herself in her books and toys.

Her gentle nature and remarkable kindness were obvious to friends and neighbors. She *never* fought; instead, she placated her mini-peer warriors and always tried to make everyone happy. When a friend tore a toy from her, she avoided confrontation and tears. "He needs it," she reassured her mother, with the knowing air of an adult.

Certain oddities began to surface when she was almost three years old. The first was an incredible compassion unsuited to her age. For example, when the neighborhood bully grabbed her by the neck, choked her, and began beating on her head, she was terrified and shaking but showed no signs of anger. "He's very unhappy," she told her mother, who had heard the fracas and hurried to her rescue.

"There's not a vindictive bone in her body," her father proclaimed. "How will she ever get along in this world, if she doesn't protect herself?" asked her mother.

A second oddity was her excessive, unheard-of generosity. She seemed *intent* on doing kind and thoughtful things for everyone. She always shared everything. A summer day did not pass without her gathering little bouquets of dandelions and wildflowers for her mother, and throughout the year, she made gifts for her friends.

A third uncommon quirk was her curious fascination with living creatures, of all sizes and shapes. "Why do many people think bugs are disgusting and crush or kill them?" she asked her mother. She was overwhelmed with grief at the mere thought of their dying.

Amore spent hours watching insects, looking at their many-shaped wings, iridescent colors, and quivering little antennae. If one crossed her path, moseying along to some unknown spot, she would go out of her way to walk around it, to spare its little life.

To her, a spider web was not a dirty mess to be swept away, but rather a marvelous, intricate pattern to be admired. If a bee or a hornet flew into her house, she raced for a cup, captured the wanderer, covered the rim with her little hand, and released the busy prisoner outdoors.

Her most bizarre oddity was her inability to see someone sad or hurt. No matter what she was doing, she *had to* stop and improve the situation *immediately*.

"She seems more concerned for others than for herself," wrote her teachers on the report card from the Happy-Tot Nursery School.

"How's she doing?" Dr. Dedicated asked Mrs. Adore, during a routine checkup, shortly after Amore's third birthday.

"She's a pleasure to have around."

"Anything unusual?"

"No, only her good heart," she began, somewhat ominously, half-joking. "It's as if she doesn't have a "self." She's so concerned about others that she puts everyone else first, before her own needs. She is unnaturally *un*selfish."

"That's not a fatal illness," he laughed. "A little unselfishness can only make this world a better place. How rare! You should be proud; you must be doing something right!"

"But seriously, have you noticed anything out of the ordinary?" he continued, with his pen poised over her chart.

"Well, now that you mention it, she frequently presses her hand to the left side of her chest, when she sees someone or something that makes her sad. If I ask her why, she says her "spot" hurts.

"Deep inside," Amore piped up. "It aches," she added, trying to describe how she felt with her as yet limited vocabulary.

Amore had been asking her mother many, many questions about the world; and she cried bitterly when she learned about unhappiness.

"What happens to a fly when it dies?" Amore queried innocently one day, when they were in the car, turning at the busiest intersection in town. "Does it go to the hospital?"

"No," answered Mrs. Adore, concentrating on the traffic, never anticipating such a conversation. She was not prepared to discuss death or unpleasant subjects with her child. Life would be hard enough later; let Amore remain free of tragedies for a while.

But Amore kept asking, and her young heart throbbed intensely. Almost every day now, her hands flew to her "spot" to soothe the intense pulsations, and frequently her face contorted with pain.

They returned to Dr. Dedicated, who detected a noticeable change. The murmur was louder and more insistent, and her heart was growing bigger. It was larger than it should have been at her age!

He monitored Amore very carefully for weeks with a portable machine, testing her heartbeat and noting its changes, while her mother kept a daily diary of activities. To everyone's surprise, the heartbeat grew stronger when Amore experienced sadness—and even stronger when she responded with one of her many acts of generosity. Successive X-rays showed a swelling, enlarging heart.

Flurries of phone calls lighted up international switchboards, and faxes fanned out across networks of fiber optic cables. The Greatest Medical Center and the Annual World Conference of Vacationing Physicians waited for further news.

"She is a strapping, healthy child," the Greatest Minds repeated. "She just has a BIG HEART!"

"An idiot could have told us that!" screamed the outraged citizens of Somewhere, who were dying for an answer to comfort Amore's distraught parents.

Meanwhile, the medical world logged the changes into its books and waited—an intolerable situation for the family. But everyone, ordinary citizen, and Great Minds were all in the same helpless position.

"Try to emphasize the Positive; distract her with happy things; avoid suffering," all agreed.

Amore's heart swelled and relaxed, palpitated and thumped, depending on what she saw or thought.

While other Somewherian kids loved to pull the tails of cats and dogs, Amore defended animals. One morning, two boys amused themselves by teasing her cat, Hearty. She intervened, protecting him with her small body. As she held him close, stroked his velvety fur, and tried to calm his desperately racing heart, he lashed out, lifted his paw, and scratched her from the top of her forehead to the bottom of her cheek, slashing her skin at the very edge of her right eye.

"Never mind," she told her distressed mother, who rushed to clean the long, deep, bloody wound. "He was just scared; he didn't mean to hurt me."

Her heart grew bigger. Curiously, however, the changes in her heart did not affect her growth or her appetite, and never inhibited her activities.

Her parents encouraged her to do whatever made her happy, including a strange new passion she developed for heart-shaped objects. She called it Heart Collecting.

It began on Valentine's Day, shortly after her fifth birthday, when her father brought home an enormous red velvet heart-shaped box filled with melt-in-your-mouth milk chocolates. Amore was allowed to help serve: she could undo the luxurious pink satin bow and tie it up again. She enjoyed tracing the curving, soft surface of the box with her fingers and squirreled it away in her room as soon as it was empty.

The family was soon filling the big heart with other cordate creations. Why the very next week, Amore bought a tiny red heart-shaped eraser and tucked it safely in her Valentine box, next to a small heart-shaped crystal her father had once given his bride.

As time passed, heart-shaped objects became the decorative theme of her room: the white satin sachet with red embroidery, the gilded music box, an antique lace doily, red gummy hearts and lollipops, fuzzy stickers, and a shiny green malachite stone carved into a heart smaller than your thumb.

She was elated when her father brought her white socks with red heart ribbons and a sweater with pewter heart-shaped buttons. She covered her bed with a heart-shaped comforter and pillows; she watered the gray-green speckled heart-shaped leaves of the plant on her windowsill; and she walked gingerly across the red and pink rug, in—you guessed it—the shape of a heart.

But try as they might, her parents could not shield her from the world. There was sadness everywhere, and the more she understood, the more her sympathy grew, and so did her poor, beating heart.

"Why do people who are mentally ill lie homeless in the streets of our cities?" she asked one evening, after watching the news on television. Her parents had many ideas, but none that satisfied her.

"Why are children hungry and starving in this world?" she added, solemnly.

Her parents sat in stony-faced silence.

"Why do people kill each other?" she continued, with an urgency in her voice, as if she had to solve the problem immediately.

Many attempts at answers, but they could find no answers.

"Why is there prejudice, hatred, and war?"

Her parents were speechless. What could they say? "It seems to me that people only *TALK* about 'loving your neighbor like yourself,'" Amore cried. "Why don't they *do what they say?*"

Dumbfounded, Mr. and Mrs. Adore tried to interpret the hypocrisy of the world, to rationalize the evil in men's hearts. They were contradicting themselves, in sentences filled with lots of "or's" and "but's." When it came right down to analyzing life's complexities, THEY DIDN'T REALLY KNOW why the world was in such a sorry, sad, miserable state. IF ONLY THEY COULD CHANGE EVERYTHING AND MAKE HER HAPPY!

Amore's heart heaved, swelled, and grew accordingly. By the time she was a teenager, there was a slight protrusion on the left side of her chest.

Because she was embarrassed and didn't want to look different from her friends, she bought large baggy sweaters, oversized jackets, extra-roomy dresses and man-sized shirts to hide her "spot." She hoped her big heart would not be noticed.

At the beach, she kept her coverall on, even when she went into the water. No one paid much attention. She was so pretty and friendly; who cared? Everyone thought she was just avoiding sunburn.

Despite her cool exterior, her inner emotional world was tumultuous. At school, she was studying world history, reading about tyrants, murderers, wars, famine, plagues, incurable illnesses, and lives of despair. She took each story to heart and was deeply moved.

"What is man doing to his fellow man and why is he making such a mess of the natural beauty of this earth?" she asked herself, obsessively.

She wept at the sad endings of the great novels and sobbed over doleful poetry. She loved music, and when she read about the death of a composer, she mourned. She struggled to find an opera with a happy ending. Amore was developing a morbid fascination with sorrow.

Sometimes, her heart felt as if it would break, tear through her flesh, rip open her skin, and fly into a million pieces!

"Is she depressed?" Doctor Dedicated asked.

A cadre of the World's Greatest Psychiatrists was summoned.

"No!" was the unanimous, resounding response. "She experiences great joy, has wonderful friendships, loves to work and play, eats with gusto, and has no trouble sleeping or concentrating. To top it off, she takes pleasure in the greatest achievements of mankind."

"She has every ingredient necessary for happiness: she is beautiful, with inner grace, many interests, and multiple talents. People love her, and she is kind to everyone, regardless of race, religion, gender, and economics. There's nothing wrong with her psychologically. In fact, the world would be greatly improved if we had more people like her!"

"She just seems to react more strongly and deeply than others to events around her," the Chief Examiner suggested, hesitantly.

What now?

"Send her to college; a change will be good for her. New scenery and different faces will divert her mind and help to reduce the pressure on her intensely responsive heart."

But college life offered no respite: she was immersed in more novels, more sad operas, more study of war and human suffering. Her emotions heaved and hoed, and her heart continued its persistent growth.

Influenced by the writings of the great Rationalists, Amore made every attempt to use her intellect to cope with life, to make "the best of this Best-of-All-Possible-Worlds."

But matters became worse shortly after graduation, when the world went to a new kind of war, one you could watch on television. Broadcasts bombarded her eyes with millions of images of bloodshed, terrified civilians, and demolished buildings. Noxious chemicals and poisonous nerve gases threatened human and animal life. Accompanying the pictures were wailing sirens and screams of terror, punctuated by humming jet engines, monotone news reporters, and gaps of deathly silence.

"Think positively," urged her mother, quoting the opinions of the great doctors.

"Try to concentrate on the beauty and majesty of the world," she added, searching for her own words. "Focus on the work of extraordinarily creative minds, on the fragility and diversity of nature's many wonders. On the mindbogglingly variety of flowers, the multiplicity of colors and patterns of butterflies, the palette of sunset, the warmth of love, and on and on . . ."

Nothing worked! She couldn't deny reality for long. Everywhere she went, the news followed her. Headlines jumped off newsstands, flashing in her eyes.

She could turn off the TV at home, but not the radios playing in the stores, blaring from car windows, and grating on her ears in restaurants. No matter where she was, there was talk, talk, talk of war, war, war.

Try as she could, there was NO escape from stories and thoughts that made her heart sore. Mankind was careening through the universe on a fiery roller coaster, and SHE FELT TERRIBLE!

One hot summer day late in August, her heart simply "burst."

Out popped a tiny red, puffy thing. There it was, sitting on her chest, pulsating gently—quite delicate and pretty. It reminded her of an inflatable valentine.

What was happening? She wondered, as she ran to her mother, who raced to the doctor, who flew to the telephone and the fax machine. Within minutes, pictures were rocketed to the Great Minds, who were startled, distressed, and powerless, as usual!

What should be done? Was the new condition dangerous or life threatening? Could the area become infected? Why was there no bleeding?

Dr. Dedicated devised a clever system to cover the area: an easily replaceable, clear plastic bag kept the tender little heart immaculate.

Once again, the watching and waiting began.

But nothing happened!

NOTHING CHANGED!

For the first time, in as long as she could remember, now that her heart was out in the open, Amore seemed to be relatively at peace. When she felt sad, the little heart fluttered. When she was calm, it stayed quiet. When she felt happy, it seemed to puff a bit. But it definitely had *stopped growing.*

Another sigh of communal relief fluttered the leaves in Somewhere's tall stately trees.

Amore sat for hours in her room, trying to understand her new "condition." Hearts were wonderful things, after all, she consoled herself. As a heart collector, she had thought a lot about their happy association with love.

"The human mind and language seem to treasure and value hearts. We have so many expressions emphasizing how important hearts are," she noted in her new diary.

She took out her thesaurus and made a list: hearts and flowers, heart's desire, heart-stirring, heartstrings, heartthrob, heart-to-heart, heart-rending, hearty, heartening, to be all heart.

"Without hearts, there would be no life, no heartfelt messages," she argued, to her mother. "Clearly, no one can be or wants to be without a heart!"

"And how negatively the world views someone who is heartless or hardhearted," she mused, trying to reassure herself. "Who wants to have a heartache? or to be heartsick, or heart-sore, heartbroken, or heartstricken? It certainly is no compliment to be described as having a heart of stone!"

But she was alone and unbearably lonely in her uniqueness.

Over and over, she listened to the opening of Robert Schumann's love-song, *Widmung*: "You are my heart." She spent many sad hours trying to console herself, playing Liszt's arrangement for piano, *Liebeslied*.

Surveying her Heart Collection which had grown over the years, Amore reorganized the cordiform knickknacks on the shelves of her white wooden bookcase. Her pent-up emotions flooded out of her reddening eyes. With steamy wet cheeks, she turned over the white teacups and mugs with little red hearts, remembering the happy days when she had found them.

Amore was surrounded by hearts: heart-dotted pencils and pens decorated her desk, and her jewelry box was overflowing with heart-shaped necklaces, bracelets, rings, and barrettes. She flopped on her bed and hugged her old teddy bear, who wore a big red felt heart on his stuffy, puffy chest.

To escape from her anguish, she tried to redirect her mind to love poetry, lovesongs, and heartfelt greetings, but the mental effort was exhausting, fitful, and unsuccessful.

Suddenly, she recoiled in horror at the idea of "wearing your heart on your sleeve." Having her heart in the open was a fact, but words now took on ominous meaning. She made another list.

What about:

"put your heart into" something?

"to have one's heart set on?"

"to find one's heart?"

"to be all heart?"

"to learn by heart?"

"to go to one's heart?"

"after one's own heart?"

Stop! She had to turn off her mind and relax. She was grateful that her heart was just "there," that it was not "on her sleeve," not "in her hand," not "in her mouth!"—that she was alive.

In the mirror, she watched the little heart on her chest puffing proudly, up and down—kind of loveable and cute, nothing disagreeable. Ever since it had "surfaced," she'd been more comfortable, less agitated by sadness. What a relief: no pounding, no pressure, no hidden agony.

She still responded to unhappy situations, but not with the drama of the past. Quite visibly, in fact: inflating and relaxing, depending on the events. But she was getting used to her new situation, beginning to accept who she was, entirely.

"I don't have much choice," she told her mother, trying to be cheerful."I can either come to terms with myself and make the best of my fate or suffer constantly. After all, what's wrong with having a loving, responsive, sympathetic, warm, obvious heart?"

But the "open" heart made her family and friends uncomfortable; she was such an anomaly. How weird, how unbecoming, how unnatural. Little by little, they avoided spending time with her. She was so . . . er . . . um . . . ah . . . ?

Life-long friends talked about her behind her back and crossed to the other side of the street when they saw her coming. The grocer was afraid to take money from her hand, fearing that he might catch a rare disease. The butcher could not bear to look at her, imagining what was under her coat. The baker tried to be polite but felt very ill at ease in her presence. Little children pointed at her knowingly. Wherever she went, tongues wagged and Somewherians found excuses to say a quick goodbye.

Forced to spend more and more time in the privacy of her own room, Amore found herself playing mental games with heart terminology. Was her case heart-breaking?   Heart-rendering?   Heart-robbing? Heart-wounding? Would it make one's heart bleed? How dreadful the words sounded!

She decided that in the case of her heart, as in other matters, people seemed to espouse one belief but to act in a diametrically opposed way. If hearts are so important, why should she be ashamed of hers?

"What is the difference between meaningful talk and empty lip-service?" she asked herself. "Does anyone really love his or her neighbor like himself? Who is really 'giving' to his fellow man?"

When she concluded that selfishness is more widespread than understanding and compassion, she cautioned her poor, tired mind.

"I'm just depressed," she thought. "Surely it is not possible that heartlessness is more common than love, that there is more talk about giving than actual giving."

In her bones, Amore knew the meaning of heartbroken, heartache, heartsickness, heart-wounding. Above all, she needed heartening. Instead, support for her vanished.

"I think you should leave town and go where no one will know your story, where you can start again," her *own* mother and father told her. "We wish you wouldn't have to go away," they added, awkwardly, "but we can't bear the social ostracism."

"We all must get out of this rut and get on with our lives," Mr. Adore peeped, wistfully.

"We have discussed the possibilities with Dr. Dedicated, who agrees that a big city would be a good place," Mrs. Adore took over. "Your moving would be best for everyone."

"But don't tell anyone about your condition," her father cautioned, fearfully.

"You know how to take care of yourself, and if you need help, there are medical experts everywhere!

Simply hide your heart and go forward," Mrs. Adore added stridently.

"It's all right, Mother," Amore answered, pretending to be calm. "I had planned to go off on my own anyway, after graduation. I'll be fine."

But inside, she felt sooooooo uncertain and unsure of the future. She couldn't and wouldn't express her feelings to her mother; she had inflicted enough suffering already.

Shortly afterwards, Amore moved to the biggest city in the country—the better to hide in—and found a tiny apartment in a sea of glass and steel skyscrapers. She knew no one.

For the first time in her life, she had no distractions. No friends to please, no flowers to pick, no family. Sitting by herself, she thought and thought.

"Why? Why me? Why have I been so cursed?" she asked herself over and over. "Why can't I be like everyone else? Wouldn't I be better off, if I didn't have such sensitive feelings?"

She watched people bustling in the streets, at the movies, at the supermarkets, everywhere. She'd never seen so many human beings in one place. They all acted as if they belonged on this earth and appeared to fit into society. Only she was an outsider looking in, one of a kind.

Amore read the want ads and found a job, where she worked conscientiously, wore her baggy clothes, and spoke very little. She went directly home every evening and declined invitations on weekends. No one could get to know her very well. She was safe. If she didn't open up to anyone, she would not have to bear one iota more of rejection.

Every day, she took a long walk for exercise. Hungry, homeless, mentally ill people begged on the sidewalks, just as she had seen on television. Others huddled in doorways and lay forlorn in the parks. She observed scores of faces pass by the waifs with glazed eyes and impassive expressions, but each dirty, disheveled, pathetic individual tugged at her heart. She didn't know how to respond. If she were to give money to all the helpless people drifting through the city, she would exhaust her entire salary within a few hours.

"Ugh!," said a pin-stripe-suited executive to his elegantly dressed wife, recoiling from a rag-draped, lame man near a concert hall one evening. "Disgusting. Why doesn't he go to work the way I do? Lazy bums. I'm not going to give any of them a red cent. They just spend it on liquor and drugs anyway."

His attitude made Amore furious. How could a human being walk indifferently past those limp, pitiful bodies strewn along icy-cold benches covered with cardboard blankets? How did entire families walk over and around pathetic mothers clasping innocent, hungry children squatting on frozen pavement?

Yes, she was an exception and an oddity: she wanted to ameliorate the condition of each and every living soul.

The next morning, she went to the bank, bought rolls of coins, and filled her pockets. No matter how small her contribution, she would do *something*. Now she would give a few cents to every poor person. After all, they were condemned to the streets, to the dangers of public shelters, and to lives without dignity. By comparison, she was enjoying and wallowing in superabundant riches.

Little by little, Amore emerged from her reclusive existence. At Thanksgiving, she volunteered to feed the hungry at a soup kitchen. But even there, among seemingly kindhearted people, she was cautious and sought anonymity.

Helping others made her feel good, whole, happy, and temporarily—even momentarily—dissipated her loneliness.

She visited a school for underprivileged children, and soon offered to plan special weekend outings to ballgames, theatrical events, and museums. Before she knew it, she was surrounded by little friends who wanted to spend time with her and adored her stories, conversation, and cookies.

As she took step after step out of her self-imposed isolation, filling free time by being useful to others, Amore met men and women with similar interests and developed a large circle of friends and acquaintances. Like the good old days in Somewhere: those who knew her came to love her, admire her thoughtfulness, and enjoy her company.

Among them was a brilliant, handsome young lawyer who had chosen a career representing those below the bottom rung of any social ladder. He was also writing a book about injustice in human history.

Amore told him almost everything in her heart, and he didn't seem upset. Quite the contrary: her thoughts, dreams, and compassion endeared her to him and made him love her and treasure her above all women on this earth.

He understood her uniqueness and appreciated her rare gifts. "Along with your good heart comes a precious human being," he reassured her. "How much nicer this world would be, if there were more people like you."

She felt a proud flutter on her chest, but she did not dare to discuss "matters of the heart."

After much time had passed, she told him her sad story, running the risk that he would shun her, as her family and everyone else had done. But the truth did not change his opinion or feelings. It endeared her to him more . . .

He told her that she was charming, original, and simply wonderful. He explained that her narrative moved him and made him love her generous, adorable heart even more. Touching her gently, he drew her close to him. With the tips of his fingers, he traced the shape of her cheeks. His lips brushed softly across her forehead and down to her lips. He put his big, strong arms around her, and passion from deep inside suffused his face. He didn't want to let her go.

"Heaven forbid that anything should happen to that marvel of a heart," he told her one evening, when he asked her to marry him. "I treasure every inch of you!"

Her parents were delighted to hear the good news. Of course, they would come to the city to meet him; there was no need for her to travel *all the way out of her way* to Somewhere!

"What luck that there is a man in the world that appreciates her and will take care of her," Mrs. Adore confided to her husband. "But what on earth is wrong with him?"

A year after their marriage, Amore called to say she was pregnant. Her parents were apprehensive. Would she be adding another human being to this world with her freakish "problem?" Was her "condition" hereditary—or just a mutation?

Months later, they arrived in time for the delivery. Dr. Dedicated had come too, in the interests of science and friendship. Holding Amore's hand, he announced proudly: "Twins! And I hear a murmur in each of their hearts."

"How wonderful! We are adding more people like you to the world," her husband said, beaming.

He bought a pink and a blue layette and took his little family home. When his wife was settled, and the twins were sleeping, he handed her a manuscript.

"Here, look at this. I can't wait to hear you read the happy ending to the children's story I'm writing."

(see Endings 2 and 3)

Ending #2

With mixed feelings, her own mother and father said, "I think you should leave town and go where no one will know your story, where you can start again. They regretted having to send their daughter away, but they could not bear the social ostracism.

"It's all right, Mother," Amore answered, pretending to be calm. "I would have been going off on my own any way, after graduation. I'll be fine." But inside, she felt soooo lonely, uncertain, and unsure of her future. She couldn't and wouldn't express her fears to her mother; hadn't she inflicted enough suffering already?

While Amore contemplated her next move, there was a long, awkward silence. Her parents waited uneasily, shifting in their chairs, crossing and uncrossing their legs. Suddenly, a sharp, persistent ring startled the little family. What a relief: someone was at the door.

"How lovely to see you," said Mrs. Adore, ushering their neighbor, the famous lawyer Shyster A. A. Prevaricator into the room.

An unannounced visit from him was a rare event indeed, because he was a VERY busy and important man. He spent his days arguing in court, his nights preparing for his endless bouts of litigation, and his weekends on many a golf course looking for new cases.

A local-home-town-boy-made-good, Shyster was one of the prides-and-joys of Somewhere. His battles put many spotlights on the tiny town, his victories belonged to each and every citizen, and his reputation cast a golden glow across their rooftops. Why almost daily, he and his statuesque wife, Sue, were pictured on the social pages of newspapers at home and abroad.

What an honor to have him descend on the Amore household.

Since Shyster became a celebrity, there had been much speculation about his initials: A.A.

Methuselah, who remembered everybody and everything, was interviewed and smiled knowingly, refusing to divulge family secrets.

An old boyfriend of Shyster's mother swore they were a code for: An Accident. One historian searched the birth records and found no middle initials. According to a fourth source, A.A. stood for Argumentative and Authoritative. According to a fifth: Avaricious and Able.

A lifetime acquaintance gave the simplest explanation: The name symbolized the happy union of *a* Shyster (his mother's family) *and a* Prevaricator (his father's name).

Shyster loved the mystery and the debate; his favorite pastimes were obfuscating and playing semantic games. So, he threw out suggestive trails of A-words, laughing and embracing the Fifth Amendment, whenever questioned. A cynical reporter grew tired of the question, with a cartoon captioned: Anal and Awe-Inspiring. Shyster responded through his public relations experts, saying he was Amused and Ascerbic.

"I have great news," Shyster told the emotionally devastated Adore family, pulling a pile of papers out of his alligator briefcase.

"I have taken the liberty of creating and exploring some unbelievable opportunities for you lucky folks. It's not every day that someone's heart breaks out, as you well know. And you know, too, how unselfish I am, how much I enjoy giving. I thought I'd surprise you, so I called a few well-placed contacts. They confirmed my wildest suspicions."

"This is quite fantastic," he chuckled, growing excited, placing the documents in neat rows. "Hollow-wood is interested. Everyone agrees with me that this is a best-selling story, if there has ever been one. It's news, it's hot, it's exotic, it's like a fable. Who would ever imagine such a happening????"

"Look here, we've already got 16 offers for books. (I say we, of course, because I would represent you. I wouldn't trust anyone else to care for your interests.)

And look here in this pile, I have 7 contracts for movie-rights; a script auction and war is brewing. And the name Amore Adore is perfect; no one would suspect it isn't fiction. We couldn't dream up a better one, if we hired Charles Dickens or Shakespeare."

"Sign here," he said, pointing to the first set of papers he had arranged on the coffee table. "Here are offers for TV and radio talk shows, lecture tours, satellite conferences, interviews, and a line of Heart Throb cosmetics which Cover Up Blemishes While Bringing Out The Real You!"

"How's that for ingenious marketing?" he added, patting himself on the back.

"And there's more: This contract is for Amore Dolls. And this one is for a pop-up children's book version of the tale. And here are the TV rights. And get this: Mugs with heart-shaped handles, with Amore's portrait on one side and with you, her devoted parents, pictured on the opposite side. This company wants to produce Amore paper cups and toothbrush sets. This one will do placemats. And this one: Pajamas with heart-pockets."

"You are going to be a star, young lady," he said, turning to Amore. "A very rich young woman! What a lucky girl!"

Mr. and Mrs. Adore fawned over their unexpected guest. "How can we ever thank you, Shyster?"

"Please, please call me Shy. What are friends for? Just put yourself in my hands, and you're safe," he said, wrapping his arms around Mrs. Adore.

"Who would have thought we could have such a happy ending?" asked Amore's father. "Our daughter has always enriched our lives, and we were so worried about her future. You are a *deus ex machina*, Shy! A genius. A miracle worker! The only thing you seem not to have thought of is the circus . . ."

"Oh, that's another possibility that I forgot to mention . . ."

Years passed; all Shyster's dreams and schemes came true. Amore lived in the limelight, swept away from Somewhere to Nowhere, the Country's capitol.

Feted and sought after, bought and sold, like an object at a slave auction of old, she was caught up in a swirl of activity. The Business Book of World Records included her every year, always on page 13, line 13. Her entourage protected her from the public, except to the extent that she wished to have contact.

Because of her economic position, she was able to help many good souls less fortunate than herself, but her advisors warned that people might "want something from her" rather than "want her for her own intrinsic merit." So, she became suspicious and learned to guard her thoughts and feelings.

Some biographers thought she lived happily ever after. Others suspected she was lonely and unhappy. As time passed and new fads and fashions replaced her, she was increasingly isolated.

But the town of Somewhere never forgot her. Standing on the Village Green is the statue erected in her honor, near the aging gazebo where it all began.

Ending #3

Amore becomes a celebrity. Everyone wants to be like her. Amore hearts are sold to be worn outside your clothing, and dolls, plus other heart-related paraphernalia bring her a fortune.

As a result, she does good for everyone in her path and in her life.

About the Author

 **Dr. Joan Thomson Kretschmer**, Artistic Director and founder of the Lyric Chamber Music Society of New York, attended Smith College, graduated from Barnard College, and received her M.A. and Ph.D. in musicology from Columbia University, where she was a Clarence Barker Fellow. She has been a music critic for *The New York Post* and has written articles about music for *The New York Times*, *Opera News*, *Stagebill*, *Keynote*, *The Greenwich Time*, and other publications. Her program notes have appeared at concerts at Mostly Mozart, at the Metropolitan Museum of Art, and elsewhere.

At The New School for Social Research, Dr. Kretschmer created and hosted Musicians on Music, a series of interviews with artists Daniel Barenboim, Victor Borge, the Guarneri String Quartet, Marilyn Horne, Zubin Mehta, Birgit Nilsson, Jean-Pierre Rampal, Peter Schickele, Andre Watts, Robert Merrill, and others. She has taught at The Juilliard School and lectured at the SUNY at Purchase and for the Metropolitan Opera Guild. At Yale University, she directed an Oral History of Electronics in Music, a collection of interviews with significant innovators in twentieth-century musical life.

In addition to writing scripts for radio and national broadcasts of The Richard Tucker Gala, she hosted Upbeat, her own classical music radio show.

A grateful student of pianist Jascha Zayde, she has performed with wind and string players from the NY Philharmonic, including Joe Robinson, Principal Oboe, and Sheryl Staples, Principal Associate Concert Master.

She was the music consultant on the award-winning film "Le Refuge" by writer/director Elliot Thomson and for *Vincent Van Gogh: A Portrait in Two Parts*.

Joan is also the author of **YONA:** *Discoveries, Doorways, and Musical Superpower* and other works.

As an active educator, she gives piano lessons and music classes to all age groups in her studio near Lincoln Center.

Visit her website at: **JoanKretschmer.com**

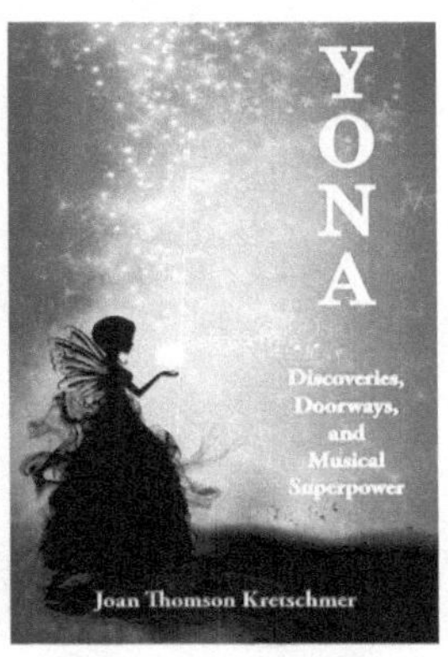

YONA: *Discoveries, Doorways, and Musical Superpower*
Joan Thomson Kretschmer

We meet Yona at age ten, an unwanted, scorned child, discovering her unique talents and beginning to exercise her special gift, the power of music. Multi Tasker is her dramatic, magic-wielding piano teacher with his Flights of Fancy, a flying piano. Her new friend, Ulysses, is a ten-year old boy who finds an abandoned, dilapidated trunk and its colorful, ebullient occupant, Gene E.

Tasker arranges for them to attend The John Brook Summer Music Festival, where they live and study in the historic mansion donated by Mrs. Goodnkind, a wealthy, benevolent role model. Daily lessons include trips and exciting adventures as well as Doorways to Understanding, a series of entryways to learning about creativity, life, nature, the arts, and values.

The tip of the iceberg of their unique curriculum includes: Music, art, talent, generosity, fear, positive thinking, leadership, science, the beauty and complexity of Mother Nature, the Moon, alleviating suffering, good and evil.